Joy Takes Root

WRITTEN BY **GWENDOLYN WALLACE**

ILLUSTRATED BY **ASHLEIGH CORRIN**

Kokila

"It's time for your grand tour," Grammy announces, reaching her hands out to Joy. Even though Joy visits her grandparents' house in South Carolina every summer, this is her first time gardening with Grammy.

"The most important thing to remember," Grammy begins, pointing out okra, spinach, and strawberries, "is that plants are our friends and our family."

Joy looks carefully at a bumblebee on the blossom of a squash plant and nods.

"The next part of the garden is filled with herbs that I can turn into medicine."

"Plants can be medicine?" Joy asks, thinking about the yucky purple liquid her dad makes her drink when she has a cough.

"Oh yes!" Grammy exclaims.

"Plants aren't the only medicine, but if you know which ones to use, they can be very helpful. You have to listen to what your body tells you."

And so Grammy shows Joy the yellowroot plants she uses when she has a cold.

She tells Joy to smell the leaves that she will dry later for tea to help her relax at night, and to touch the leaves of her calendula flowers, which she will make into a balm for her dry hands and feet.

"But now, it's time for you to plant some seeds of your own." Grammy kneels down and Joy sits next to her. "The first step," Grammy says, closing her eyes, "is to take a few deep breaths. During these breaths, it's important to think about the ancestors who came before us and the ways they took care of this same soil."

"All of their love is in you, and you will pass it on to the people who come after us."

Joy closes her eyes and breathes deeply through her nose. She smells the sweetness in the air and feels her thoughts start to slow down a little bit.

Then Grammy puts her hand on her chest. "Earth has a heartbeat just like you do, little one. Can you feel the Earth's rhythm along with your own?"

Joy places one hand on her chest and feels her heartbeat.
"Not really," she replies.

Grammy opens her eyes and chuckles. "That's okay.
Listening takes practice, my dear."

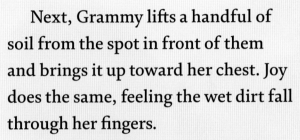

Next, Grammy lifts a handful of soil from the spot in front of them and brings it up toward her chest. Joy does the same, feeling the wet dirt fall through her fingers.

"When we garden," Grammy says, "we have to put our intention into the soil, something you are wishing for and want to happen. Breathe your intentions from your heart, through your hands, and into the ground."

Joy closes her eyes and breathes her hopes out over the dirt.

"What did you wish for, Grammy?" Joy asks.

"You'll soon find out, my dear," Grammy replies, and then takes a handful of different seeds out of her pocket. Some are round and black, and others are tan and curved. Joy had no clue seeds came in so many shapes and sizes. "There is just as much life in each seed as there is in your body." Grammy places the seeds in a line in the soil. Joy covers them gently, thinking of everything her body is made of.

Grammy picks up her watering can and hands it to Joy. Then she smiles and says, "Each drop of water holds the memories of all the water before it. Sometimes, if we focus on it, water can help us remember things too."

As she listens to the sound of the water hitting the ground, Joy remembers the song Grammy used to sing as she gardened. Joy begins to hum, and Grammy joins in.

Once Joy and Grammy are done watering the seeds, they sit down and take five more breaths. "Let's thank the soil and the seeds and the sun and our ancestors for letting us work with them today," Grammy says. Joy does, and she also adds some thanks for her grandmother.

"Would you like some ginger snaps now?" Grammy asks. Joy nods and they both walk to the kitchen, where Grammy brings out a heaping plate of cookies and mugs of warm, sweet tea.

The next day, before Joy gets in the car to go home, Grammy gives her some seeds.

"Thank you, Grammy. I don't know if I can take care of these as well as you do, though." Joy tries to give them back, but Grammy shakes her head.

Grammy kneels down in front of Joy and whispers, "Yes, you can."
Grammy points at Joy's heart and says, "There are things your body
knows in here"—she moves her finger to Joy's head—"that you don't
know up here yet."

As soon as she gets home, Joy plants the seeds.

She remembers to slow down
and breathe her intentions into the soil.

As she waters the little mounds, she hums Grammy's song. And then she waits. And waits. And waits.

Two weeks later, she sees that her first plants have popped out of the soil. As the days pass and her plants grow, Joy sits with her green friends and tries to listen to all of nature's rhythms.

Joy smiles as she understands exactly what Grammy's wish was.

Joy puts a hand on her chest and realizes she can hear the heartbeat
of the Earth just as loud and clear as her own.

Thank
you,
Grammy.

To my grammy, who was the first person to teach me about the magic of plants.
—G. W.

To my grandparents. Thank you for all of your wisdom and love.
—A. C.

KOKILA
An imprint of Penguin Random House LLC, New York

First published in the United States of America by Kokila, an imprint of Penguin Random House LLC, 2023

Text copyright © 2023 by Gwendolyn Wallace
Illustrations copyright © 2023 by Ashleigh Corrin

Visit us online at penguinrandomhouse.com.

Library of Congress Cataloging-in-Publication Data is available.

Manufactured in China

ISBN 9780593406786

1 3 5 7 9 10 8 6 4 2
TOPL

This book was edited by Sydnee Monday and designed by Jasmin Rubero.
The production was supervised by Tabitha Dulla, Nicole Kiser, Ariela Rudy Zaltzman, and Caitlin Taylor.

Text set in FS Brabo Pro

The art for this book was created digitally with textured brushes and hand-drawn elements.